19

The Adve

THE ISLAND

All eight titles in the Adventure series are available from Piper books

The Island of Adventure
The Castle of Adventure
The Valley of Adventure
The Sea of Adventure
The Mountain of Adventure
The Ship of Adventure
The Circus of Adventure
The River of Adventure

Also available by Dave Morris in The Adventure Squad *series*

The Castle

The
ADVENTURE
Squad

THE ISLAND

Dave Morris

based on Enid Blyton's
T HE I SLAND OF A DVENTURE

PIPER
PAN MACMILLAN
CHILDREN'S BOOKS

First published 1994 by Pan Macmillan Children's Books

a division of Pan Macmillan Publishers Limited
Cavaye Place London SW10 9PG
and Basingstoke

Associated companies throughout the world

ISBN 0–330–335693

Copyright © 1994 Dave Morris

The right of Dave Morris to be identified as the
author of this work has been asserted by him in accordance
with the Copyright, Designs and Patents Act 1988.

Enid Blyton is the trademark of Darrell Waters Ltd
© Darrell Waters Ltd 1994

All rights reserved. No reproduction, copy or transmission
of this publication may be made without written permission.
No paragraph of this publication may be reproduced, copied or
transmitted save with written permission or in accordance with
the provisions of the Copyright Act 1956 (as amended). Any
person who does any unauthorized act in relation to
this publication may be liable to criminal prosecution
and civil claims for damages.

1 3 5 7 9 8 6 4 2

A CIP catalogue record for this book is available from
the British Library

Phototypeset by Intype, London
Printed and bound in Great Britain by
Cox & Wyman Ltd, Reading, Berkshire

This book is sold subject to the condition that it shall not,
by way of trade or otherwise, be lent, re-sold, hired out,
or otherwise circulated without the publisher's prior consent
in any form of binding or cover other than that in which
it is published and without a similar condition including this
condition being imposed on the subsequent purchaser.

THE ADVENTURE SHEET

See if you can get all five good ideas.

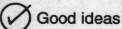 Good ideas

You are only allowed three mistakes,
so be careful!

 Mistakes

This is a gamebook. In a normal book, you just read the story from beginning to end. But in a gamebook, you get the chance to affect the outcome.

You will need a pencil. As you go through the adventure, sometimes you will be told to put a tick or a cross on the Adventure Sheet. (This is on the page opposite. The circles are for you to put ticks or crosses in.) A tick means that you have made a good choice, whereas a cross means you have done something wrong. If you have read *The Island of Adventure*, you ought to bear in mind that Jack, Philip, Dinah and Lucy-Ann are not infallible – they do make mistakes themselves, so don't think you just have to remember what they did in the novel and copy it!

It is possible to succeed even if you make one or two mistakes, so do not give up too soon. But if you enjoy a real challenge, see if you can get right through to the end of the adventure without getting any crosses at all. If you can do this then you deserve to be a member of the Adventure Squad yourself!

Are you ready to begin? If so, turn to page **1**.

It is the school holidays. Jack Trent and his younger sister Lucy-Ann have come to stay with their friends Philip and Dinah Mannering. They are very impressed by their first sight of Philip and Dinah's home, which is a great ramshackle manor-house perched half-way up a cliff by the sea.

"The house is called Craggy-Tops," says Philip as they get out of the car. "On stormy nights the waves dash high up the cliffs and you can hear the spray against the windows."

"It all sounds very thrilling," says Lucy-Ann. Then she gives a shiver and moves closer to her brother. This is because the sinister handyman Joe, who has driven them from the station, has just turned to them with a black look.

"Don't you go out along the cliffs on stormy nights – or on any nights, come to that!" growls Joe. He hauls their bags out of the back of the car and stomps off down the path leading to Craggy-Tops.

"He's a gloomy fellow, isn't he," says Jack. "What was that about not going along the cliffs at night?"

"Oh, don't bother about Joe," replies Philip with a laugh. "I think he's a bit simple, actually. He seems a bit gruff and strange, but there's no harm in him really."

Lucy-Ann watches the burly figure of the handyman as he goes down the path ahead of them. She isn't convinced. There is something about Joe that frightens her. Turn to page 11.

The boys wait in pitch darkness as Joe turns the key in the lock. The door opens with a rusty creak and Joe enters carrying an oil lamp. He does not notice Jack and Philip, who are hidden behind a stack of crates.

A hollow cough breaks the silence. It is Kiki the parrot, imitating Philip's Uncle Jocelyn, but Joe does not know that. He does not know about the secret passage to the beach, and he thought the cellar was empty. He drops his lamp in fright and it breaks, plunging the room into utter darkness. Joe bolts back up to the kitchen.

When Philip is sure Joe has gone, he lights the candle. "Look, he's left the key in the door," he says to Jack.

Philip slips the key into his pocket. It might come in handy later. Put a tick next to the picture of the key on your Adventure Sheet.

Before Joe can pluck up the courage to come back, the two boys return along the secret passage to tell Lucy-Ann and Dinah what they've found. Turn to page 32.

After breakfast they take a walk along the clifftops. It is a warm day, with gusts of wind blowing inland and bringing the delicious clean smell of brine.

They have brought a packed lunch, and around midday they clamber down to a secluded spot on the beach to have their picnic. But first they decide to go for a swim. It is not long before Philip, who is the best swimmer of the four, has reached a large rock jutting out from the water. As he climbs up to take a breather, he sees something that gives him quite a surprise:

"Look over here! It's a boat!"

Sure enough, there is a sailing boat pulled up on a flat shelf on the seaward side of the rock. "Somebody must have hidden it here," says Jack when he swims over. "I wonder who?"

After lunch they stroll further along the beach until they spot a ramshackle hut perched in a cleft in the cliffs. "Do you think that's where the boat's owner lives?" says Lucy-Ann.

There is one sure way of finding out. Do you think they should go up to the hut and knock on the door (turn to page 13), or turn around and go home (turn to page 23)?

They set off at a brisk pace, but Lucy-Ann notices quite soon that Joe is following. "We mustn't lead him to Bill's hut," she says.

Jack nods. "I'm sure Bill prefers his privacy. That's why he hides his boat out of sight of the shore."

"Oh dear," says Dinah, glancing back at the determined figure of the handyman striding along about a hundred metres behind them. "It was a mistake to let Joe see us going this way."

"What a pity!" squawks Kiki, fluttering around Jack's head.

Put a cross on your Adventure Sheet. If you now have three crosses, turn to page 70.

As long as you don't yet have three crosses, you can decide if the children should turn back (turn to page 54), continue along the cliffs towards Bill's hut (turn to page 44), or go for a swim (turn to page 34).

s the sun sinks in the west, it clearly outlines the grim brooding bulk of the Isle of Gloom. "People used to live on the island in the old days," Philip says. "My uncle told me there were copper mines out there, or something."

"No one goes there any more because of the jagged rocks just off the shore, though," adds Dinah. "Ships give it a wide berth."

"So there's no chance of us visiting it," concludes Lucy-Ann, slightly relieved.

"But it would be an exciting adventure, if only we could!" says Jack.

Turn to page 15.

"We could go to the Isle of Gloom in Joe's boat," suggests Dinah the next morning.

"Perhaps there's someone stranded out there," says Lucy-Ann. "A shipwrecked sailor, I mean. He might have been signalling for help."

Philip is still puzzled. "But in that case, who did Jack see signalling back? Was it Joe, or someone else?"

"I can't believe dopey old Joe knows Morse code!" says Dinah with a laugh.

"Talk of the devil," says Jack, nodding through the window. They look out to see Joe clumping up the path towards his car. It is his day to go shopping in town. This is their chance to borrow his boat and sail out to the island – if you think they ought to. If they should, turn to page 65. If they would be wiser to stay on dry land, turn to page 55.

They spread the map out on the ground and kneel down to study it. It shows a maze of underground galleries and passages. "It's a good job we've got this," says Philip. "We'd soon get lost without it."

Choosing a passage at random, they set out to explore the mines. Their candles make the walls gleam with a greenish colour like oxidized copper. Then, emerging into a large cavern, Lucy-Ann makes an interesting discovery. She holds it up for the others to see.

"A pencil stub!" says Philip. "So people *have* been down here recently."

Look at the Adventure Sheet. If there is a tick beside the picture of a hut, turn to page 17. If not, turn to page 27.

S oon they reach a chamber lit by a shaft of daylight from above. It is the way they came in. Scrambling up the ladder, they emerge into the open air with great relief.

There is no sign of Jack. "He must still be trapped down there," says Dinah. Lucy-Ann cannot help crying; she is worried about her brother.

"We'd better go back to the mainland and get help," decides Philip. Turn to page 18.

Aunt Polly becomes quite ill at the news. She has to be helped to a chair, where she sits looking pale and unwell. "Oh dear, this really is dreadful," she says.

Lucy-Ann starts to cry. Deep down she had hoped that something could be done to whisk her brother to safety. Now, seeing Aunt Polly so distressed, she cannot stop her tears.

Hearing the noise, Uncle Jocelyn comes lumbering out of his study. When he is told what has happened, he is no help at all. He just stands there blinking and asks: "Jack who? The boy with the parrot? He's been staying here, has he?"

Bill takes charge. He puts through a call to the police. Soon a helicopter comes thundering across the moor and touches down on the clifftops. Turn to page **19**.

They reach the shaft. A faint glimmer of daylight trickles down from far above. But their jubilation soon turns to despair when they see that the bottom part of the ladder has been hacked away. They cannot climb out.

"Joe wasn't taking any chances," says Bill. "He made sure that even if we got out of the cell we'd still be trapped."

As he says this, there is a muffled explosion from deep in the mines – followed by a dull roaring sound. "That was the dynamite!" cries Philip. "The sea's pouring in!"

The children are very frightened, but Bill tells them to stay calm. "We still have a chance," he says.

Positioning them right under the shaft, Bill waits till the sea water comes gurgling up the tunnels and starts to rise around them. "Now, start treading water!" he says.

As the water level rises, it carries them all up the shaft. Soon they reach the upper part of the ladder – Joe's men only bothered to chop the lower rungs away – and are climbing to safety.

Turn to page 101.

When Philip explains to his Aunt Polly that he has brought two friends home for the holidays, she is none too pleased. "Fancy springing guests on me like this!" she says sharply. "Where will they sleep? We've no room, really, and you know I have enough on my hands looking after your Uncle Jocelyn."

Uncle Jocelyn is an eccentric man who spends all his time working on a history book about this part of the coast. Philip knows that Aunt Polly is overworked, but he promises that they will all help her with the household chores.

Suddenly Jack's pet parrot, Kiki, flutters over and settles on Aunt Polly's shoulder. Everyone winces, thinking that this is the last straw. Now Aunt Polly will surely send Jack and Lucy-Ann home. But then Kiki squawks: "Poor Polly, poor Polly." Hearing this, Aunt Polly cannot help smiling. At last she relents, and agrees that Jack and Lucy-Ann can stay. They are delighted!

The next day it is time for Joe's weekly trip into town for the shopping. "I'll be gone for hours," he tells the children. "While I'm gone, fetch up some water from the well."

If you think they should do as Joe says, turn to page **21**. If they ought to ask him to take them shopping with him, turn to page **31**. If they spend the day exploring, turn to page **41**.

Joe opens the door and scowls at them. The flickering light of the lamp he's holding illuminates his face from below, making him look huge and sinister. "How did you get in here?" he demands to know.

Jack looks at Philip and then shrugs. What harm can there be in telling Joe the secret, he thinks. "There's a passage down to the beach under that trapdoor," Jack blurts out.

"Trapdoor, eh?" mutters Joe. "Well, you know, I never noticed that before. What clever kids you are. Now, beat it!"

Put a cross on your Adventure Sheet. It was a mistake to let Joe know about the passage. The boys hurry back to join Lucy-Ann and Dinah and tell them what they found. Turn to page 32.

Put a tick next to the picture of a hut on the Adventure Sheet.

The door opens. There is a man dressed in shorts and an open-necked shirt. He has a strong pleasant face and he greets the children in a booming merry voice. "Hello there," he says. "Coming visiting, eh?"

"We saw your boat on the rock," says Philip, pointing back over his shoulder. "At least, I suppose it's yours."

"Yes, it is," replies the man. "I'm Bill Smugs, by the way. Who are you?"

They introduce themselves and tell him they come from Craggy-Tops. Bill is quite surprised. "I know the house. I didn't know there were any children staying there."

"We're down for the school holidays," chips in Lucy-Ann.

Bill smiles at her. "Cornwall is a great place for a holiday, isn't it!"

Lucy-Ann nods, then wrinkles her brow in a frown. "It would be even better if we could go out in a boat, but Joe the handyman is a bad-tempered grouch and won't take us."

"Well, *I* don't mind taking you out in my boat," says Bill.

If you think they ought to take him up on the offer, turn to page 33. If you think they ought to be getting back to Craggy-Tops, turn to page 43.

With Philip and Jack leading the way, they locate the secret tunnel and make their way up to the house. The hidden room in the cellar is stocked with ample supplies of food and drink. "Joe must be expecting a siege!" jokes Dinah.

When they open the door leading to the main part of the cellar, they find that Joe has stacked empty boxes in front to hide it. Obviously he is up to something that he doesn't want anyone to know about. "I expect he wonders what happened to the key," muses Philip.

"Can't you shut the door?" chirps Kiki the parrot.

They go up through the kitchen and sneak out the back way, keeping to the path along the cliffs. There is no sign of Joe. "I expect he's still keeping a watch on the cave," says Lucy-Ann.

Jack laughs. "Eventually he ought to realize that we aren't coming out. Won't he be baffled!"

Turn to page 64.

Jack cannot get to sleep that night. He is too excited, as he is thinking about all the rare birds that must live on the island. He lies awake for what seems like hours. Finally he cannot stand it any longer – he gets up and goes to the window, hoping for a glimpse of the island.

Outside, the night is totally dark. There is no moon, and although Jack can hear the soft surge of the waves he cannot see anything at all. He might just as well be looking into a coal bunker. Then he catches a glimpse of something – a light, winking on and off like Morse code.

Jack rubs his eyes and looks again, but now the light has gone. It seemed to be out to sea due west of Craggy-Tops, where the Isle of Gloom lies. Jack has just about convinced himself that it was a trick of his imagination, and is about to go back to bed, when he sees *another* light out of the corner of his eye. But this light is coming from the direction of the clifftops. Someone must be signalling to the island!

Jack decides to go outside for a closer look. As he pulls on his clothes, Kiki flutters over and settles on his shoulder. She wants to come with him. If he should let her, turn to page 25. If he should leave her behind, turn to page 35.

As they get close to the beach, they catch sight of the girls waving to them. Rowing the boat to its usual mooring-place by the jetty, they get out and tie it securely.

"Joe will never know we took it," says Philip. "Now, let's get back to the house and we'll tell you all about our adventure!"

"Don't forget to wipe your feet, now," mutters Kiki as they reach the door.

Turn to page 55.

"Not just any pencil," says Dinah. "Oh, don't you notice *anything*, Philip? That pencil belongs to Bill. I saw it in his shack the other day."

"Crafty old Bill," says Philip with a grin. "You see what's going on, don't you? Men are working these mines in the hope of finding the odd bit of copper that the old miners missed. I expect Bill's their lookout, and he must bring their supplies in his boat."

"And the light Jack saw was probably him signalling to his friends out here. Of course!" says Dinah.

Before he can say any more, there is the sound of footsteps and a lantern beam blazes out of the darkness. Two rough-looking men are standing there. Ignoring the children's protests, they seize them and push them along the tunnels, turning first left and then right, until they reach a door.

"Get in there!" says one of the men, shoving them through into a small room. He slams the door and locks it.

Philip hammers on the door. "Let us out. We're friends of Bill!"

"And who's he when he's at home?" replies the man. "No, you wait in there till the boss gets back."

Turn to page 37.

L ook at the Adventure Sheet. If you have ticked
the picture of a hut, turn to page 28. If not, turn
to page 38.

The police go out to the island, and a few hours later they return with Jack. He is safe and sound, if a little shaken by his ordeal. Kiki sits on his shoulder and keeps saying: "Isn't it dark, Kiki? Isn't it dark, Kiki?"

It soon becomes obvious that Bill Smugs isn't really a bird watcher. He is a Special Branch officer, and his real name is Bill Cunningham. He gathers them all around and tells them what has been going on. "We suspected a gang of crooks was operating in this area," he says. "Their hideout was on the island. We've rounded up most of them, but their boss got away. And you'll never guess who the boss was – Joe, your strange handyman!"

That's the end of the adventure. You did quite well in helping to catch the crooks, but you could have done better. If you want to have another go, rub out any ticks and crosses on the Adventure Sheet and turn to page 1.

"No, no!" yells Bill, running after the children. He catches hold of them and manages to calm them down enough to explain that they can't escape along the tunnel. "It's below sea level," he explains, "so it will flood along with the mines. We have to get up one of the shafts down from the island."

Going the wrong way has wasted precious time, and the dynamite will blow any minute. Put a cross on your Adventure Sheet. If you now have three crosses, turn to page 70. As long as you don't yet have three crosses, turn to page 10.

The well is in a small yard at the back of the house, beside the rocky cliff. Lucy-Ann peers down the deep shaft and watches as Philip winches up a pail of water.

"I'm surprised it isn't salty," says Jack. "Doesn't the well shaft go down further than sea level?"

"It must do," agrees Philip. "I expect the water is rain that gradually trickles down from the clifftops. It's pure fresh water – and deliciously cool on a hot day."

After they have fetched up enough water for the cooking and washing, the four friends decide to take a stroll along the shore. Turn to page 41.

The boys nip back into the passage just seconds before Joe opens the door. They can hear him striding about in the cellar above their heads, muttering to himself.

"He's a strange one, and no mistake," whispers Jack.

"Ssh!" replies Philip. "We don't want him to hear us."

Quietly they return back down the passage to where Lucy-Ann and Dinah are waiting.

Turn to page 32.

A storm blows in that evening and rain rattles against the window panes all night long. The next day is blustery and cold, so the children entertain themselves at home with some games that Philip and Dinah find in a cupboard.

After a day or two the weather brightens up again. Dinah packs a hamper with sandwiches and fruit. "We can have another picnic," she says.

"Yes," agrees Lucy-Ann. "It'll be nice to get out after being cooped up in the house for days on end."

Look at the Adventure Sheet. If there is a tick next to the picture of a hut, turn to page 80. If not, turn to page 53.

When they come back out of the cave, Joe is still there watching them with his baleful stare.

"This is hopeless!" groans Philip. "How are we going to slip away and see Bill?"

"We could just set off along the cliffs," suggests Jack. "After a while Joe will get fed up with following us."

If you think that's a good plan, turn to page 4. If you think it is too big a risk, turn to page 54.

Jack walks along the cliff path in complete darkness. He cannot see any trace of a light now. Suddenly a torch beam stabs out of the dark, dazzling him, and an instant later a powerful hand closes like a vice on his arm. In the torchlight he sees Joe's scowling face.

"What are you doing up here?" hisses the man, shaking him roughly.

"I saw a light," gasps Jack, "and I came to see what it was."

"You came snooping, you mean!" says Joe. "Well, I'm going to give you a good hiding that'll make you think twice in future."

He raises his hand. Before he can strike, Kiki launches herself at him and gives him a very painful bite on the wrist. He gives a yelp of pain and lets Jack go.

Jack loses no time in running back along the path. Joe is too busy fending off the angry parrot to chase after him. When he is safely at the kitchen door, Jack calls Kiki back to him and they hurry up to the tower room. "That was a narrow escape," pants Jack. "Thanks, Kiki!"

Turn to page 6.

After landing and hauling the boat up the beach, the boys set out to explore the island. Jack is impressed by the profusion of birds. There must be hundreds. There are many species that he has only seen before in books. But they are not very tame, flying off smartly whenever the boys come near.

"That is odd!" says Jack. "You'd think that birds on a deserted island would be tame, since they'd never have learned to fear man."

Philip says nothing. He has made a more astonishing discovery. After staring at it for a while, he calls his friend over. "Look here, Jack! There's a hole right down into the ground!"

They drop a stone down, but there is no sound of a splash, so it cannot be a well. "I think it must be very deep," says Jack.

Looking around, they find more holes. When they notice the remains of ladders going down into them, Philip realizes what they are: "Mine shafts! My uncle said that there used to be copper mines out here."

Near one of the shafts is a pile of empty meat and fruit tins. Not all of them are rusty. Now Jack and Philip are sure that someone else has visited the island recently. They return to the boat and cast off. Turn to page 16.

Picking their way across the cavern, they pass some large bundles wrapped in brown plastic. Philip tears the plastic covering on one and peeks inside. "It's paper!" he says in surprise. "Loads of blank paper."

"What's that funny noise?" asks Dinah suddenly.

They all stop to listen. A continuous clunking and clattering noise echoes distantly down the warren of tunnels.

"It doesn't sound quite like digging machinery," says Philip.

"How would you know?" scoffs his sister.

Philip glares at her. "There would be drills and things, wouldn't there? And a sound like breaking rocks – hammers and so on."

"Just hold it right there!" says a gruff voice from behind.

Whirling, the children see two rough-looking men with lanterns. Before they have time to run, they are grabbed and hauled off down a tunnel. The men take them first right and then left, then shove them through a door and lock it behind them.

Philip finds himself battering on the door before he has recovered from his surprise. "Let us out!" he yells.

But the only answer is a hoarse rattle of laughter.

Turn to page 37.

The sun is setting when they tie up the boat at the jetty, and by the time they reach Bill's hut it is quite dark. They knock but there is no reply. Philip pushes the door open. The hut is empty. "He's not at home!" groans Dinah.

In the gloom at the back of the hut, a small red light is winking on and off. They go over and find a radio with a microphone attached to it.

"It looks like someone's signalling," says Philip, turning to the two girls.

Should they talk into the radio (turn to page 48), leave it untouched and wait outside the hut (turn to page 58), or go back to Craggy-Tops and tell Aunt Polly what's happened (turn to page 38).

At the bottom of the well, just above the level of the water, is the mouth of a gaping tunnel. It is slimy and evil-smelling. "I don't think I shall ever be happy to drink water from this well again after this," says Philip with a grimace.

The group of them set off along the tunnel. It is cramped and the air tastes stale. In places the tunnel slopes up or down so sharply that the people who excavated it cut crude stone steps to make the going easier. The steps are so slimy that it is difficult to stay upright, though. Several times they slip and fall, taking some hefty bruises in the process.

It seems to take hours. The children try not to think about the huge weight of rock above their heads – and, beyond that, the relentless surge of the sea.

The tunnel walls begin to show a greenish tinge, showing that they are nearing the island. "We must be very quiet from now on," Bill warns them. "We don't want those men to capture us too."

As he says this, they hear footsteps scraping on the dank stone floor of the tunnel ahead. Someone is just around the next bend. Quickly Bill flicks off his torch, plunging them in darkness. Everyone holds their breath. Then someone suddenly comes round the corner and blunders smack into Philip, almost knocking him over. Stumbling back, Philip puts out a hand to steady himself and feels his fingers close around a heavy rock.

What should he do? If you think he should hit the stranger with the rock, turn to page 49. If he should hold on to him until Bill can come over to help, turn to page 59.

Jack loses no time in fetching Bill and showing him the secret tunnel. "My boat's been sabotaged," says Bill. "If we're to rescue your sister and your friends, this tunnel is our only route."

The two of them set off along the tunnel. It is cramped and the air tastes stale. In places it slopes up or down so sharply that crude stone steps had been cut to make the going easier. These are so slimy that it is difficult to stay upright, though. Several times they slip and fall, taking some hefty bruises in the process.

It seems to take hours. Finally the tunnel walls begin to take on a greenish tinge, showing that they are under the island. They make their way quietly through the mines, hiding whenever they see any of the crooks, until they reach a locked door. Bill presses his ear to the door and after a moment he nods, smiling. Trying a bunch of lock picks, he manages to get the door open. Lucy-Ann and the others are relieved to be let out, but Bill warns them to be quiet.

He herds them down a tunnel. "We should be safe enough now," he says. "It's time to let you in on the secret. These men are crooks – very dangerous men. I've been trying to catch them for weeks. Fancy them having their hideout here on the Isle of Gloom!"

Suddenly a bright torch beam stabs out of the darkness and a voice says: "Figured it out at last, eh, copper? What a pity you'll never get to tell your mates!"

The children's hearts skip a beat. A voice they know only too well! Have you already guessed the chief crook's true identity? Turn to page 79 to see if you're right.

"There's not much point," says Philip, shaking his head. "I got in the car with him once, and he just hauled me out. For some reason he doesn't like taking us into town with him."

All the same, Lucy-Ann screws up her courage to ask Joe to give them a lift.

To no avail. "I can't be bothered with you kids," Joe says sullenly. Before Lucy-Ann can say anything else, he has gone striding off towards the car. "And be sure to get in some water," he calls back over his shoulder before driving off.

"How very odd!" says Jack.

"He's a strange one, all right," agrees Dinah. "And lazy. I think Aunt Polly would sack him, except she'd never get anyone else to work here for the money."

Joe told them to get some water from the well. If you think they should, turn to page 21. If not, turn to page 41.

Jack and Philip share a bedroom in the high tower of Craggy-Tops. During the night, Jack is woken by the sound of Kiki shifting on her perch. The full moon is shining in through the window. Jack sits up and yawns, and is just about to turn over and go back to sleep when a thought strikes him. Perhaps he will be able to see the Isle of Gloom in the moonlight. Getting up, he goes over to the window and gazes out to sea. What he sees there gives him quite a surprise.

"Philip, wake up!" he calls. "Come and look at this!"

Philip gets up and wanders sleepily over to the window. "What is it?"

"A sailing boat," says Jack, pointing. "I think it must be Joe's."

"Whoever it is, he's coming towards the shore. Let's go down and see," suggests Philip.

Do you think they should go down to investigate? If so, turn to page 60. If you think they ought to stay safely indoors, turn to page 50.

They spend the rest of the afternoon sailing in Bill's boat, the *Albatross*. It is nearly as big as Joe's boat, but Bill handles it with great dexterity.

Through the haze, they can just see the dim outline of the Isle of Gloom out to the west. "Can we go there?" Jack asks Bill.

Bill does not answer straight away. He just sits grinning with his eyes half-closed and the sun and spray in his face. He looks like an old sea captain. Then he says: "Well, I'm sure it would be exciting, but I'm afraid we can't. There's a ring of rocks right round the island that make it very dangerous."

The time passes all too quickly, and soon they have to sail back. As Bill pulls the *Albatross* up on to the shelf of rock, Dinah asks: "Why do you keep it here, Bill?"

"You mean 'her', not 'it', Dinah," replies Bill. "Boats are always called 'her'."

It is only when they're halfway back to Craggy-Tops that Dinah realizes Bill never answered her question. But he has promised to take them sailing again, and next time she is determined to find out the secret. Turn to page 23.

The children make parcels of their clothes and go swimming out through the waves. Joe can only stand on the beach and stamp his foot angrily. He is not a very good swimmer and would never have a chance of keeping up with them. Also, he cannot spare the time.

Philip is the first to reach the rock where Bill Smugs keeps his boat. After they have rested there for a few minutes, they swim to shore and climb the path to Bill's hut.

Turn to page 64.

Jack walks along the cliff path in complete darkness. He cannot see any trace of a light now. Suddenly a torch beam stabs out of the dark, dazzling him, and an instant later a powerful hand closes like a vice on his arm. In the torchlight he sees Joe's scowling face.

"What are you doing up here?" hisses the man, shaking him roughly.

"I saw a light," gasps Jack, "and I came to see what it was."

"You came snooping, you mean!" says Joe. "Well, I'm going to give you a good hiding that'll make you think twice in future."

He raises his hand, bringing it down in a sharp stinging slap across the side of Jack's head. Fortunately, before the spiteful man can hit him again, Jack manages to squirm free and run back to the house. As he scurries back to bed, he realizes he is lucky to have got away with no worse than a thick ear.

It was a mistake to get caught by Joe. Put a cross on your Adventure Sheet. If you now have three crosses, turn to page 70. As long as you don't yet have three crosses, turn to page 6.

J ack happens to turn the map over. There are some interesting markings on the back. Taking it over to the window, he holds it up to the sunlight. It looks like a diagram showing a maze of shafts and tunnels.

Slowly, Jack manages to puzzle out the faded script across the top of the diagram. "It shows the mine workings on the Isle of Gloom!" he says.

"That might explain the light you saw, Jack," thinks Lucy-Ann. "There might be people out there looking for gold nuggets!"

"Copper, actually," says Philip. "But I suppose it is possible."

The next day is Joe's day off. They know that he will drive into town. Usually he does not get back to Craggy-Tops until late afternoon. Philip suggests borrowing Joe's boat while he's gone and sailing out to the island to investigate.

If you think they should, turn to page 45. If not, turn to page 56.

They hear footsteps going away. It is only now that the children realize that there are just three of them in the room. "Where's Jack?" says Lucy-Ann.

"I think Kiki got lost and he went back for her," says Philip. "Maybe he'll realize we've been caught and go for help. Meanwhile, we ought to think up a plan to escape."

"I've an idea," says Dinah. "When those men come back, we pretend we've been overcome by the stale air. We'll gasp as though we're choking. They might take us out into the passage where the air is fresher."

Philip raises his eyebrows. "And what then . . .?"

"I'll kick over their lantern and we'll run off as fast as we can!"

Look at the Adventure Sheet and, if there is a tick next to the picture of a torch, turn to page 90. If not, turn to page 47.

The police are called in. They arrive the next morning, asking the children some questions and then taking a helicopter out to the island. Philip is taken along to show them the mine shafts.

Lucy-Ann goes out with Dinah to get water from the well. Both want something to take their minds off worrying. Imagine their surprise when they hear Jack's voice shouting up from the bottom of the well! They lower a rope and soon he is climbing up to safety. He looks grimy and a little shaken, but Kiki is perched calmly on his shoulder looking to and fro as though nothing were amiss.

Soon the police return with Philip. "There was a gang of crooks on the island," they say. "We've rounded up most of them, but their ringleader escaped."

This is the end of the adventure. You did quite well in helping to catch the crooks, but you could have done better. If you want to have another go, rub out any ticks and crosses on the Adventure Sheet and turn to page 1.

Bill disappears into the darkness at the bottom of the well. When he has not returned by noon, the children start to get very worried. "There might have been a cave-in," says Philip. "Bill might be trapped down there."

Dinah sees that Lucy-Ann is worried sick. "No, that's not very likely," she says. "If the tunnel's been there for two hundred years it's hardly likely to collapse now."

"Well, Bill might have been captured by those men out on the island," says Philip. "I'm calling the police."

He is glad but a little surprised that he has no trouble convincing the police that his call isn't a hoax. Within an hour, a helicopter comes thundering out of the sky and touches down on the cliffs above the house. A uniformed police officer listens to the children's story and nods. "Bill shouldn't have gone off without calling us," he says.

They watch the helicopter take off and sweep out towards the Isle of Gloom. "Oh dear," says Dinah. "I think we've got Bill into trouble."

Put a cross on your Adventure Sheet. If you now have three crosses, turn to page 70. As long as you don't yet have three crosses, turn to page 19.

The map clearly shows a safe passage through the reef, just in line with a high hill in the centre of the island. Jack steers safely through, and with a whoop of delight the boys tack in towards the shore.

Turn to page 26.

Jack takes out his binoculars as they walk along the beach. He gets so involved in looking out to sea that he almost forgets his friends are there. "One day, Jack's going to be a famous ornithologist," Lucy-Ann tells the others proudly. "That's a person who studies birds."

But suddenly Jack catches sight of something that takes his mind off the gulls wheeling overhead. "It's an island!" he cries. "I can just see it through the haze."

"That's the Isle of Gloom," Dinah tells him. "No one ever goes there. Usually it's covered in mist and you can't see it at all."

Jack lowers the binoculars. His face is full of excitement. "Joe has a boat, hasn't he? Could we get him to take us out to the island, do you think? There might be dozens of rare birds."

"You've seen what Joe's like," says Philip. "He's not likely to want us in his boat."

"We could just borrow the boat while he's in town," suggests Dinah. If you think they should, turn to page 51. If it wouldn't be wise, turn to page 61.

Jumping out from behind the rock, the two boys whoop like Apaches on the warpath. Joe is so taken aback that he loses his balance, teetering for a moment on the edge of the jetty with his arms spinning crazily. Then he falls into the water with a huge splash.

Philip and Jack laugh so much at this that they have to hold on to each other to stay standing. But the grins are wiped off their faces when Joe swims back to the jetty, spluttering water, and gives a roar like an angry lion.

It wasn't a very good idea to antagonize Joe. Put a cross on your Adventure Sheet. Now the boys are going to have to run for it if they are to avoid a thrashing. Should they run to the caves (turn to page 62) or back up the path to Craggy-Tops (turn to page 72)?

"**W**ell . . ." says Philip, "maybe some other time."

"Whenever you like," agrees Bill, nodding.

As they head back home, Dinah gives her brother a push. "Why did you have to go and say that?" she demands. "I'd have loved a ride in his boat!"

Lucy-Ann is not so sure. She casts a nervous glance out to sea and says: "I think Philip's right. It's a bit too windy today."

Dinah glares at her. "You need a bit of wind to go sailing, you know!" she retorts.

Maybe it would have been a good idea to get to know Bill Smugs. Put a cross on your Adventure Sheet. If you now have three crosses, turn to page 70. As long as you don't yet have three crosses, turn to page 23.

Afew minutes later, they begin to think that they have shaken Joe off. "I can't see him any more," says Jack, looking back along the clifftop.

"He probably got bored and went back to the house," says Philip. "Look, there's Bill's car. Let's see if he's at home."

Just as they are making their way down the path to Bill's hut, a few pebbles come clattering down from the top of the cliff. Looking up, they are horrified to see Joe glaring down at them. In his hand there is a gun!

Hearing the children's shouts, Bill comes out of the hut. He is just in time to see Joe scowl in hatred and rage before turning and running off back along the cliffs.

"You kids had a narrow escape," Bill says. "That was Joe Kerr, a very nasty criminal. I suspected he was running his gang of criminals in the area – but I never guessed he was working as the handyman at Craggy-Tops!"

"And we led him straight to you!" wails Dinah. "Oh dear, Bill, have we spoilt your plans?"

"I'm rather afraid you have," Bill says sorrowfully. "I shall call in the local police on my radio. Unfortunately, Joe and his gang will be long gone by the time they get here."

The adventure didn't work out very well this time, but you can try again and see if you can do better. Rub out any ticks and crosses on the Adventure Sheet, then turn to page 1.

The next morning, they make themselves a picnic and tell Aunt Polly they will be out all day. As soon as Joe has driven off, they rush down to the jetty and row out to sea. Once the sail is up, a gust of wind sends them skimming swiftly towards the haze-covered island. Plumes of spray fly off the choppy waves.

"We've got to be careful of the sunken reef around the island," says Philip, consulting the map, "but the safe passage is clearly marked here. We just have to steer level with the big hill, then head straight for shore."

"We might dodge the rocks," replies Philip, "but I think we're going to miss the island altogether! The current's too strong!"

Look at the Adventure Sheet. If you have ticked the picture of a boat, turn to page 46. If not, turn to page 75.

Letting down the sail, they take turns over the oars for the last difficult stretch in towards the island. Soon they are pulling the boat up on to the shore. Then, with Jack striding off in the lead gazing at the hundreds of sea-birds, they set out to explore.

Dinah points at a deep shaft leading down into the ground. "Look, there's a ladder," she calls to the others.

Jack nods. "Yes, it's an old mine shaft. The ladder looks fairly new, though, so I suppose that proves that people are still interested in the mines."

"Surely they were all worked out long ago?" says Philip.

"I suppose there's always the chance of a nugget that someone missed," says Jack. "Come along, then." And with that he sets off down the ladder.

Lucy-Ann is not sure about going down the shaft. It looks very deep and dark. But she is not keen about being left behind, either, so she follows the others.

They reach the bottom, and Dinah lights a candle. "Creepy, isn't it?" she murmurs. "Don't you go picking up any spiders or things like that, Philip!"

They pick a direction at random and set out to explore the mines. Look at the Adventure Sheet. Is there a tick next to the picture of a map? If so, turn to page 7. If not, turn to page 96.

At long last the sound of footsteps approaches the door. The bolt is shot back and the door opens. A big man with a patch over one eye looms in the doorway, outlined by the lantern on the floor behind him. He has a jug of water in one hand and a plate of biscuits in the other. He is quite taken aback to see the three children lolling weakly around the cell and gasping for breath.

"The air's bad in here . . ." groans Philip.

The man tugs them to their feet and hustles them out of the cell. Philip sees his chance. Reeling as if he is too ill to stand, he suddenly lashes out a strong kick at the lantern. It shatters and the light goes out. Philip grabs the hands of the two girls and they all dash off before the startled man can stop them.

It is difficult to keep one's sense of direction in the dark. The children feel themselves at a junction in the tunnel. Should they go left (turn to page 77) or right (turn to page 87)?

Philip flicks a switch and a voice crackles out of the radio: "Y2 calling L4."

"Hello, er, Y2," says Philip into the microphone. "Are you calling for Bill Smugs? He isn't here."

"Who's that?" replies the voice cautiously.

"My name's Philip Mannering. I'm looking for Bill myself, but he's not home."

There is no reply. Should they leave now (turn to page 68) or wait for Bill to show up (turn to page 58)?

P hilip swings the rock around. There is a thud and a groan, and he feels his mysterious attacker slump to the ground.

Bill switches his torch back on. But to Philip's dismay, instead of one of the unpleasant men he met earlier, it is his friend Jack who is lying on the ground in front of him! Blood is spilling from a graze on his brow, but luckily Philip only caught him a glancing blow with the rock.

Bill comes over and hands Philip the torch, then sets about tearing his shirt into strips to bandage Jack's cut. He cleans it with saliva first. "It's a good job you're not badly hurt," he says to Jack as the boy's eyes flutter open.

Jack winces. "I've got a bit of a headache, though. Next time, Philip, you ought to find out who you've got hold of before you go belting them!"

There is no doubt it was wrong to hit Jack. Put a cross on your Adventure Sheet. If you now have three crosses, turn to page 70. As long as you don't yet have three crosses, turn to page 69.

The two boys spend the rest of the night wondering whether it was really Joe they saw in the sailing boat. "Why would he go out at night?" says Jack as they go down for breakfast.

"Who knows?" says Philip. "You've seen for yourself that he's a bit simple-minded."

Joe is in the kitchen when they walk in. Philip goes straight up to him and boldly asks: "Were you sailing your boat last night, Joe?"

Joe gives him a long heavy-lidded stare and finally replies: "Of course not. And don't you go nosing about after dark, neither!"

Turn to page 3.

They get into Joe's boat and row it out to sea, but soon they realize they've bitten off more than they can chew! The current catches the boat and carries it far out from the shore. Philip and Jack struggle to get the sail up, but only succeed in getting it hopelessly tangled.

By a stroke of luck they are spotted by a trawler whose captain calls the coastguard. A lifeboat is sent out to pick up the four children. It is dark by the time the lifeboat reaches them, and they are miserable, cold and hungry.

The coastguard returns them to Craggy-Tops. Aunt Polly is relieved to see them unhurt, but furious at all the trouble they've caused. The next day she sends Jack and Lucy-Ann back home, and that is the end of the adventure.

If you want to try again and see if you can do better, turn back to page 1.

The boys see Joe unload several boxes of rubbish and a few dustbin sacks that clatter as if they are full of empty cans.

"Where's he been?" whispers Jack. "And where did he get all that rubbish from?"

"There are more empty food tins and milk cartons than we'd eat our way through in a fortnight," says Philip. "It's very strange."

Joe takes the rubbish sacks and heads off up the path. Once he is out of sight, the boys hastily return to Craggy-Tops. The next morning, when they go down for breakfast, Joe is emptying the dustbin outside the back door. "I'm going to have a bonfire," he replies sullenly when they ask what he is up to.

Turn to page 3.

While out swimming, they take a look at the rock where they found the mysterious boat. It is still there. Philip notices something else. "The hull's wet," he says. "Someone must have been out in it quite recently, as it would soon dry off in the sun."

Jack looks around, but there is no one in sight. "I wonder who it belongs to," he says.

"And why he leaves it here," adds Dinah.

As they get home, Joe lurches out from the garden at the back of the house and blocks their way. He has a pail of water from the well. "Where have you four been all day?" he asks in his sullen gravelly voice.

What should they tell him? If you think they should mention the boat they found, turn to page 84. If you think they should ignore Joe and just walk past him into the house, turn to page 54.

Aunt Polly has been complaining of a headache all day, and by teatime she is looking very pale and tired. "I think I've been working too hard," she says. "It isn't good for me, what with worrying about all the bills and how to make ends meet."

"Poor Polly!" announces Kiki.

"That parrot is the only one who sounds at all sympathetic," sighs Aunt Polly. "I know she hasn't the slightest idea what she's saying, but at least she gives me a scrap of comfort."

Dinah feels very sorry for her hard-working aunt. "Why don't you go and have a lie down, Aunt Polly?" she says.

"All right, but you'll have to make your uncle some coffee and sandwiches, Dinah. Will you do that?"

Dinah is a little nervous of her strange Uncle Jocelyn, who rarely comes out of his book-lined study. But she assures her aunt that she will make his supper.

Jack gazes out of the window as it gets dark. "It's going to be a crystal clear night," he says. "I reckon we could see the island from the tower room."

"Let's go up and see," says Lucy-Ann.

They are all excited at the prospect. So excited, in fact, that there is a good chance that Dinah will forget all about Uncle Jocelyn's supper. If you think she'll go up to the tower room with the others, turn to page 5. If you think she would take care of the supper first, turn to page 94.

The next day, Lucy-Ann sits at the table with her chin perched on her fists. "Oh, I'm bored!" she says grumpily. "What shall we do today?"

"How about a picnic?" suggests Philip.

"Or a swim?" says Dinah.

"Not again!" wails Lucy-Ann.

Look at the Adventure Sheet. If there is a tick next to the picture of a map, turn to page 36. If not, turn to page 56.

L ook at the Adventure Sheet. Have you put a tick beside the picture of a hut? If so, turn to page 66. If not, turn to page 76.

At long last the sound of footsteps approaches the door. The bolt is shot back and the door opens. A big man with a patch over one eye looms in the doorway. He has a jug of water in one hand and a plate of biscuits in the other.

Philip shines the torch into the man's one good eye. Instead of being dazzled, he just laughs. "I've just come from a brightly lit cave," he says. "Your feeble torch isn't going to dazzle me!"

"You thug!" snaps Philip. "Let us go!"

The man's laugh turns to a snarl. He throws the water over Philip and backs out of the room, slamming the door in the children's faces. "You'd better learn some manners or you'll go thirsty," they hear him snarl.

Put a cross on your Adventure Sheet. If you now have three crosses, turn to page 70. As long as you don't yet have three crosses, turn to page 67.

Someone is coming up the path from the beach. It is Bill. He shines his torch into the hut and is astonished to see the children waiting for him. He is even more astonished when they blurt out the story of their escapade on the island. Though he looks quite angry at first, his mood changes when he hears how Jack is still trapped on the Isle of Gloom.

"That is bad news," he says grimly.

"But, Bill," says Lucy-Ann, "I don't understand. Aren't those men friends of yours? You can just tell them to help us find Jack, can't you?"

Bill pats her head. He does not give her a straight answer because he doesn't want to worry her. "We'll get your brother back, Lucy-Ann," is all he says.

Turn to page 78.

Bill switches on his torch and shines it over Philip's shoulder. The battery is starting to give out, but the beam is still strong enough to show that the person who has come blundering along the passage is Jack.

"Am I glad to see you!" cries Jack.

"I could say the same," replies Bill with a relieved smile.

Turn to page 69.

Jack and Philip quickly get dressed and hurry downstairs. Letting themselves out quietly, they take the path leading to the beach.

The sail of Joe's boat is plainly visible in the moonlight. They can also see Joe and, beside him in the boat, a cargo consisting of several boxes.

They hide behind a rock and watch Joe let down the sail and row the last fifty metres to shore. As he is tying the boat up at the jetty, Jack has an idea. "Let's jump out yelling and give him a fright!" he says.

If you think that's a good idea, turn to page 42. If you think they should stay hidden, turn to page 52.

The next day they explore the caves at the bottom of the cliff. Philip's uncle once told him that the caves were used by smugglers. Now they are empty except for seaweed, crabs and starfish.

With only a couple of candles, the interior of the caves is dark and forbidding. Lucy-Ann wants to stay outside. "If the tide came in while we were inside the caves, the entrance would be flooded and we'd be drowned," she says.

"No, we wouldn't," argues Dinah. "The caves are quite big, and there are holes leading to upper caves further up the cliff. There would be enough air until the tide went back out."

"I don't want to get trapped even for that long!" retorts Lucy-Ann. If you think she's right, turn to page 81. If you think they should explore the caves, turn to page 71.

With Joe lumbering after them in a red rage, the two boys make for the caves. In the moonlight the cave entrance is just a blotch of inky black shadow. The tide is coming in and the water level is up to their knees, but one glance back at Joe is enough to send them fleeing into the cave.

Look at the Adventure Sheet. If you have a tick next to the picture of a key, turn to page 82. If not, turn to page 92.

They watch from the shop window until Joe is safely past. "Wouldn't he have got a shock if he'd seen us!" chuckles Philip.

"Yes," says Dinah, "but how would we have explained it? I don't think we ought to let him know about Bill."

They soon find the hotel, where Bill treats them to a magnificent meal ending with huge sundae glasses filled with three flavours of ice cream. Afterwards, the four children are so full up that they can hardly walk. However, luckily they can doze off in the car, feeling the warm splashes of sunlight flickering across their faces.

Bill covers his car with the tarpaulin and waves to the children. "Come again soon and we'll go fishing," he calls after them.

Turn to page 83.

Today Bill takes the boat as close to the Isle of Gloom as he has ever been. The sea is quite rough, sending spurts of water up off the submerged rocks surrounding the island. "I can see dozens of different species of birds!" cries Jack, looking through his binoculars. "Can we land on the island, Bill?"

But Bill is adamant. "It's too dangerous. The boat doesn't even need to hit a rock. If we just capsized because of the choppy waves, there'd be an even chance of ending up impaled on the rocks."

"But there are some really rare birds!" protests Jack.

"Rare, eh?" says Bill with a grin. "Just as well we won't be clumping ashore and disturbing their nests, then."

He pulls at the tiller and the boat veers around. Once they are safely out of the crashing waves near the island, Bill relents a little and lets them take turns at steering the boat. Soon they are quite expert sailors.

Put a tick next to the picture of a boat on the Adventure Sheet. Then turn to page 74.

Jack and Philip insist on taking the boat out alone. Lucy-Ann has mixed feelings about this. On the one hand she is nervous about the idea of going in the boat, on the other she does not want to be parted from her brother.

Dinah is furious. "Why should you two have all the fun?" she fumes. "You think girls can't do anything that boys can do!"

Philip is just about to make a sharp reply that will enrage her even more, but Jack calmly points out the wisdom of the plan. "If we all go out and then the boat got swept away, there'd be no one to alert the coast-guard," he says.

At last Dinah is convinced. She unties the boat and gives it a push, and the two boys row out until they are clear of the shore. Then they raise the sail and steer out towards the Isle of Gloom.

Foam spurts up off the submerged rocks close to the island. "We'll have to be careful," warns Philip as Jack turns the tiller, "or we'll come a cropper."

Look at the Adventure Sheet. If there is a tick next to the picture of a map, turn to page 40. If not, turn to page 85.

I t occurs to the children that perhaps their friend Bill Smugs might be interested in hearing about the unexplained lights that Jack saw at night. Lucy-Ann has complete confidence in Bill. "He'll know what to do," she says.

If they should go and tell him, turn to page 86. If not, turn to page 76.

All hopes now rest with Jack. He soon finds Kiki, but just as he is looking around to see where the others went he hears footsteps. They definitely belong to adults. Pressing back out of sight behind one of the wooden posts supporting the tunnel roof, he watches two rough-looking men go by.

"We'll need more purple ink," says one.

"I'll let the boss know," replies the other. "But he'll probably be too busy figuring out what to do with those kids we caught."

Once they're gone, Jack comes out of hiding. It sounds as if the men have captured the others. Jack scratches his head. Whatever can those men be up to? Nobody ever needed ink for mining with, that's for sure!

After wandering through the tunnels for ages, he finds himself in a long passage that must run under the sea bed. Jack realizes that he is nowhere near the island. He presses on – the only place the tunnel can lead is to the mainland! It is hot and stifling, and so narrow in places that Jack feels as if he's been buried alive.

At last he feels a waft of fresh air on his face. He emerges from the long tunnel to see a glint of daylight above. He is at the bottom of the well behind Craggy-Tops! Fortunately there are rungs leading up the shaft of the well, and soon Jack is clambering up into the open.

"Lucy-Ann and the others are still trapped on the island," he tells himself. "I must get help."

Look at the Adventure Sheet. If there is a tick next to the picture of a hut, turn to page 30. If not, turn to page 100.

I t is a mistake to head back to Craggy-Tops without talking to Bill. Put a cross on your Adventure Sheet. If you now have three crosses, turn immediately to page 70. As long as you don't yet have three crosses, read on.

Later that evening, Bill shows up at Craggy-Tops. The children guess that the person who was calling on the radio must have told him about their visit to the hut. Aunt Polly has already gone to bed and Uncle Jocelyn is closeted in his study as usual, so there is no one to disturb them as they tell Bill their story. "Aunt Polly doesn't know Jack's missing yet," says Philip. "We didn't want to worry her."

Bill nods. "We'd better see about rescuing Jack before she finds out, then."

Turn to page 78.

They are all delighted to see Jack safe and well. Lucy-Ann hugs him. Truth to tell, Jack himself is the happiest of all. He was beginning to think he might be lost underground for ever.

"I've got to tell you what I've found!" says Jack. "I think the men there aren't miners at all. In fact, I'm pretty sure they're crooks. I saw a cave full of stacks of £20 notes. They must have stolen it!"

"Ah, just as I thought!" says Bill when he hears this. "No, I don't think they stole it, Jack. It's not real money, you see. I suspect they've been printing counterfeit notes."

Suddenly a bright torch beam stabs out of the darkness and a voice says: "Aren't you the clever one, eh, copper?"

The children's hearts skip a beat. That is a voice they know only too well . . .

Perhaps you have already guessed the villain's true identity. Turn to page **79** to see who it is.

Three mistakes are all you are allowed. You must end the adventure here – but there's nothing to stop you going back and having another go. You ought to do better next time. Just rub out any ticks and crosses on the Adventure Sheet, then turn to page **1**.

Gingerly, holding their candles up, they step into the cave. It smells of wet rock and salty seaweed. Suddenly Lucy-Ann gives a horrified shriek, because her brother has disappeared right in front of her.

Philip leans forward with his candle. "Oh, it's only a hole in the ground, under the carpet of seaweed," he says. "Are you all right, Jack?"

"I'm fine," Jack calls up. "There's a tunnel here. Shall we see where it goes?"

Philip is all for it, but Dinah reminds him of the danger. "What if the tide should come in?"

"Oh, the tunnel slopes up above sea level," calls out Jack. "We'll be fine. You girls wait here for us."

Dinah folds her arms. "You're a pair of idiots if you go off along that tunnel!"

If you agree they shouldn't, turn to page 81. If you want to see where it leads, turn to page 91.

Despite his size, Joe is a powerful man and he soon catches up with the two terrified boys. "Ow!" yelps Jack as Joe twists his arm. "You'd better not hurt us!"

"Hurt you?" says Joe, a slow evil smile gradually spreading across his face. "Of course not! I'm just going to take you out to the Isle of Gloom."

"What's going on there, Joe?" asks Philip as they are forced into the boat. He is frightened, but he tries not to show it.

"Never you mind," snaps Joe as he casts off.

The two boys are taken into deserted mines on the Isle of Gloom. There are a lot of rough-looking men here. Joe locks the boys in a storeroom. After some time, they hear the men packing up their belongings. Then Joe's voice calls through the door: "My pals and I are moving to a new hideout. So long."

"What about us?" shouts Philip in panic.

"Oh, once we're well away maybe I'll call the coast-guard and tell 'em you're here," replies Joe. "But it might take a day or two, so don't hold your breath. And next time you'll know not to poke your noses into things that don't concern you!"

That is the end of the adventure. But, whereas Jack and Philip can only wait for the coastguard to turn up and rescue them, you can try again and see if you can do better this time. Just rub out any ticks and crosses on the Adventure Sheet, then turn to page **1**.

Joe's jaw drops as soon as he sees the children. He cannot imagine how they could have got to town when he saw them only a couple of hours ago at breakfast. There are no bus stops anywhere near Craggy-Tops.

Anxious to get to the bottom of the mystery, Joe swerves his car into a narrow parking space and hurries across the road towards the children. Instead of waiting for him, they hurry along the road to the Royal Court Hotel and duck inside.

Joe is baffled. How could they afford even a cup of coffee in such an expensive place? He sets foot on the steps, but sees that the doorman would never allow him in with his rough unshaven face and handyman's clothes. "Go away, you old tramp," says the doorman.

Inside the hotel, the children tell Bill all about it. They have a good laugh over lunch, thinking of Joe pacing up and down in front of the hotel waiting for them to come out. After they have eaten their fill, they leave by the hotel's back entrance and are soon heading back to the coast.

"Poor old Joe!" says Jack, laughing. "He'll never figure it out!"

The others laugh too, except for Dinah. "I don't think we should have let Joe see us," she says. "It would be bad if he learned about Bill. He might badger Aunt Polly to stop us from visiting him."

Turn to page 83.

On the way home, Jack is deep in thought.

"What is it, Jack?" asks his sister.

He frowns. "Well, I've been thinking about it, Lucy-Ann, and I'm pretty sure I saw a Great Auk on the island."

"A Great Auk," says Philip, overhearing this. "They're extinct, aren't they?"

"Everyone thinks so," says Jack. He suddenly stops and looks out to sea. "Just think what it would mean if we found a bird that was supposed to have died out."

"Well, we can't go to the island in Bill's boat," Dinah says. "We promised him."

Jack slowly nods. "Not in Bill's boat," he agrees.

Turn to page 54.

Astrong gust of wind catches the sails, turning the boat out to sea. The tiller jerks out of Jack's hands. The children are flung flat as the boat lurches to one side. For one long dreadful moment they fear it is going to capsize.

"We've got to get the sail down!" cries Jack. "Then we can row back to shore."

They fumble with the sail, but by the time it is furled there is no sign of dry land. In all directions they can see nothing but water.

It is almost dark before the coastguard finds them. A searchlight shines down from the motorboat and soon they are hoisted aboard. By this time they are cold, forlorn and frightened.

"Your aunt called us," one of the coastguards tells them. "She's worried sick."

"Don't worry," groans Philip. "We've learned our lesson. We'll never go to sea again . . ."

This is the end of the adventure. Why not try again and see if you can do better next time? Just rub out any ticks and crosses on the Adventure Sheet, then turn to page 1.

That evening, Dinah takes Uncle Jocelyn a cup of tea in his study. She notices that the cup he was taken at lunchtime has gone cold on his desk. It looks as though he forgot to take so much as a sip from it. Then she sees a stale sandwich from the previous day protruding from under a stack of papers. Uncle Jocelyn really is absent-minded!

As Dinah clears up the debris of Uncle Jocelyn's earlier snacks, she asks: "What do you know about the Isle of Gloom, Uncle?"

"Used to be copper mines out there," he mutters without looking up from his work. "All the copper's gone now, of course."

"How could they be sure they got every single nugget?" she asks.

He glares at her as though her ignorance of the subject is nothing short of a crime. "There might well be one or two nuggets – or whatever form copper is found in. But it would hardly pay to have a team of miners working night and day just for a bit of copper worth a hundred pounds or so, would it?"

Dinah hurries back to the others. Full of excitement, she blurts out what she's learned. "If we could find even fifty pounds' worth of copper, it would be such a help to Aunt Polly in paying the bills," she says.

"Agreed!" cries Philip. "Tomorrow is Joe's day off. We'll take his boat out to the island!"

Turn to page 45.

So far so good. "I think we're on the right track," whispers Philip, feeling his way along the wall.

Behind, in the darkness, they can hear the man bellowing with rage. "His friends will soon turn up with a new lantern," says Dinah. "Hurry, Philip!"

Philip stops. They have reached a side tunnel branching off to the right. Should they take the side tunnel (turn to page 8) or go straight on (turn to page 97)?

"Someone has sabotaged my boat," Bill tells them. "I found the bottom had been smashed in."

"If we want to get to the island we'd better borrow Joe's boat," says Dinah.

"That's good thinking," agrees Bill. "We won't bother asking him, though. All in all, from what you've told me I'd say he's a pretty nasty customer."

They are in for a shock when they go down to the jetty. Joe's boat isn't there.

"He must have sailed off to the island himself," says Philip. "Where else would he go at this time of night?"

"The pieces of the puzzle are beginning to fall into place," says Bill. "And I'm afraid I don't like the picture they're making one bit!"

Turn to page 88.

It is Joe. He is standing there in the passage, shining his torch right into their faces, and in his other hand he has a gun. Before they can even think of a plan, he has called his men.

"When I smashed up your boat, I never thought you'd find the tunnel under the sea bed," says Joe to Bill Smugs. "Too bad for you that you arrived too late."

Bill and the children are led to a storeroom with a lock on the door. As they are ushered inside, Bill turns and growls: "My colleagues have my report. You can clear out, but they'll come here and find the evidence, and sooner or later we'll track you down."

Joe shakes his head. He snatches Bill's fading torch out of his hand and says: "They'll never find a shred of evidence, copper. Know why? Because we've rigged dynamite to blow the tunnel, that's why. Ten minutes after we've gone, the sea's going to come flooding through these mines, covering our tracks nicely."

"At least let the children go," says Bill in a different tone.

"Can't do it," says Joe. "They know too much. And in any case – " he swings the door closed – "I don't like 'em!"

Left in darkness, they listen to Joe's evil laughter as he locks the door and walks away.

Look at the Adventure Sheet. Have you put a tick by the picture of a torch? If so, turn to page 89. If not, turn to page 99.

As well as a boat, Bill Smugs has a car, which he keeps under a tarpaulin at the top of the cliff. When he shows it to them the boys in particular are very excited. "It's a Mercedes!" cries Jack.

"Ah, so you aren't only interested in birds, then," Bill says with a chuckle. "All right, who wants to come into town with me?"

They are all keen for a chance to see the town and do some shopping. It would take hours to walk into town from Craggy-Tops, but it is a ride of only twenty minutes in the car. After Bill has parked, he tells them that he has some business to see to. "Can't we come?" asks Lucy-Ann.

"It will be very boring for you," he says. "You can meet me later for lunch. Let's say one o'clock at the Royal Court Hotel."

"Bill must be very rich," says Dinah as they watch him walk away.

"Maybe he's just particular about how he spends his money," says Philip. "He doesn't have much of a home, after all!"

They buy a torch for exploring the caves, as well as some film for Jack's camera. Put a tick next to the picture of a torch on the Adventure Sheet. As they leave the shop, a car horn blares out. Turning, they see Joe driving along the high street with his usual scowl on his face. He hasn't noticed them.

"Let's go back in the shop until he's gone past!" says Lucy-Ann. If you agree, turn to page 63. If you think they shouldn't bother about Joe, turn to page 73.

They walk on further along the shore. Just as Jack is sweeping his binoculars around the jagged coastline, Philip spots a tiny speck far out to sea. "Hey," he says, tugging Jack's sleeve, "have a look and see what that is."

Jack turns the binoculars out to sea. "It looks like a man in a boat," he says, puzzled. "It can't be Joe, can it?"

"I don't see who else it *could* be," says Dinah. "Other than Joe, there's nobody with a boat for miles around."

Lucy-Ann is bored. "It's almost time for tea," she says. "Let's go back."

Jack lowers the binoculars and shrugs. "Yes, okay. Anyway, that must be Joe, mustn't it?"

But when they get back to the path leading up to Craggy-Tops, they see that Joe's boat is still moored in its usual place. "What a mystery . . ." says Dinah.

Turn to page 32.

Blundering along in the darkness, Jack and Philip find the secret tunnel leading from the cave up to the house. As they head along it, Jack whispers: "Let's hope Joe doesn't follow us."

But Joe has no intention of entering the cave in pitch darkness. He does not know about the secret tunnel, so he thinks the boys are trapped. He has no idea that, at the same time that he is relishing the idea of them shivering inside the cold dank cave, they are actually letting themselves out of the cellar and going back up to bed.

The next morning, Jack and Philip come down to breakfast to find Joe looking very tired and grumpy. It is obvious that he must have waited all night outside the cave. He is astonished to see the two boys obviously just out of bed. "Where did you come from?" he growls, glancing out of the window in the direction of the cave.

"From the tower, of course," says Philip innocently. "You know that's where our bedroom is, Joe."

"You been in your bedroom all night?" says Joe, puzzled.

"Of course! Where else?"

When Joe stamps outside to collect some firewood, the boys cannot help dissolving into laughter. Turn to page 3.

Over the next few days, Joe starts to get suspicious. For one thing, he cannot understand how the children are forever bringing home marvellous catches of fish. "You haven't been out in my boat, have you?" he asks them.

"Of course not," replies Philip. "How would we even know how to sail it, seeing as you won't teach us?"

Joe nods, lip curled in a sneer. "That's all right, then. But I can't think where you get off to each day."

"Oh, here and there," Jack says breezily.

"Weren't you ever young and carefree, Joe?" says Dinah.

Joe glowers at her. "I wasn't always up to no good, like you lot," he replies testily.

He takes to watching them closely, sure that they are up to something behind his back. "Oh dear," wails Lucy-Ann to the others. "How can we slip away to see Bill now?"

If they should go off along the cliffs as usual, turn to page 4. If they ought to go to the caves, turn to page 93.

No sooner have they told Joe about the boat than he gives a great exclamation and goes racing off down the beach towards his own boat. The children watch, puzzled, as he puts out to sea.

"Where's he off to?" says Jack.

"I don't know," says Philip. "But I've got a feeling we did the wrong thing by telling him about the other boat."

"Oh dear," says Lucy-Ann as they all go up to the house.

Philip is right; talking to Joe was a bad idea. Put a cross on your Adventure Sheet. If you now have three crosses, turn to page 70. As long as you don't yet have three crosses, turn to page 54.

White foam splashes up from the water, clearly marking where the waves are crashing into submerged reef.

"I think I see a gap in the rocks," says Philip.

Jack cranes his neck to look. "Oh yes, where there's no spray. It's rather narrow . . ."

"If we steer carefully, we ought to get through all right," Philip thinks.

Should they risk it? If so, turn to page 95. If they ought to turn back, turn to page 16.

They hurry along the cliffs to Bill's hut. At first he seems very interested in what they've come to tell him, but then he only says: "Well, Jack, I expect you saw the light from a ship out to sea."

"But it looked like Morse code," says Jack.

Again Bill is interested. "Really? Do you know Morse code? What did it say?" But when Jack shakes his head, Bill laughs and says: "It was probably carried by a sailor on deck, and when he turned it just seemed to you as though the light was flickering in code."

"What about the light on the cliffs?" puts in Philip.

Bill shrugs. "Oh . . . it could have been a trick of the moonlight."

Disappointed, they head back to Craggy-Tops. "I really thought Bill would be more excited by our news," moans Lucy-Ann.

Turn to page 76.

It must be a wrong turning, because they are soon hopelessly lost. "If only we could find Jack," wails Lucy-Ann.

They try to retrace their steps, but as they return to the fork in the tunnel they are grabbed by two men with lanterns and hauled back to the cell. The rogue with the eye-patch is waiting with a mocking leer on his face. "Didn't get very far, did you?" he jeers. "Now, get back in there, and don't bother trying any more tricks. You really can choke to death, for all I care!"

The door slams shut, sealing them in. Put a cross on your Adventure Sheet. If you now have three crosses, turn to page 70. As long as you don't yet have three crosses, turn to page 67.

As they trudge disconsolately back into the kitchen, Aunt Polly puts her head round the door. She has her hand pressed in front of her eyes because the light makes her headache worse, so she does not see Bill.

"Dinah, is that you?" she says, squinting. "Be a dear and make your uncle's cocoa. I have to go back to bed."

Should Dinah do as her aunt asks (turn to page 98), or should she tell her that Jack's missing (turn to page 9)?

"If only I could see what I'm doing," sighs Bill, "I could pick the lock on that door in no time!" There is a click, and a beam of light illuminates the narrow rock-walled room. "Will this do?" says Philip, smiling. It is the torch he bought when Bill drove the children into town.

Bill delves into his pocket and produces a bunch of odd-looking keys, pins and files. "Sometimes it's useful for the gamekeeper to know the poacher's tricks," he explains as he bends down to work on the lock.

After a minute or so, the lock gives a click and the door swings open.

"Well done, Bill," says Dinah. "But hadn't we better hurry? When the dynamite goes off, this whole place will be flooded!"

Should they run towards the shafts leading up to the island (turn to page 10), or back in the direction of the secret tunnel to the mainland (turn to page 20)?

I've got another idea," says Lucy-Ann, holding up the torch. "The men will surely bring us some water, at least. When they do, why don't we dazzle them with the torch and run past?"

If they should try Lucy-Ann's plan, turn to page 57. If it's a better idea to pretend to be ill, as Philip suggested, turn to page 47.

It is a long narrow climb up the passage, and the air is stale. Both Philip and Jack are frightened, but they both go on because neither wants to be the first to suggest turning back. Kiki the parrot is just as nervous, but she hangs on to Jack's shoulder.

At last they reach a short flight of steps cut into the rock. Above their heads, in the wavering candlelight, they can see a trapdoor. "We must be under the house," says Philip.

Sure enough, once they have pushed up the trapdoor they find themselves in the cellar of Craggy-Tops. But it is not any part of the cellar that Philip has ever seen. All around are crates of canned food and bottles of beer.

They soon find that there is no easy way out of this part of the cellar. They come to a heavy door, but it is locked. Just as they are resigned to returning along the secret passage, they hear footsteps on the other side of the door.

"It's Joe," says Philip as he hears the handyman's distinctive tuneless whistling. "What shall we do?"

If you think they should blow out the candle and hide, turn to page 2. If you think they should call out for Joe to unlock the door, turn to page 12. If they ought to go back down the secret passage, closing the trapdoor behind them, turn to page 22.

Jack and Philip are trapped. They flounder around in the dark until they get so cold and bedraggled that they have to return to the cave mouth. There they get a nasty surprise. The tide has come in, flooding the entrance. They are trapped inside the cave all night.

They are only able to emerge when the tide goes out in the morning. They slog wearily up the path to the house, where Joe is waiting at the kitchen door with a broad smirk on his face. "You boys must've got up early for a walk, eh?" he says gloatingly before going inside for his breakfast.

Getting stuck in the cave wasn't very clever. Put a cross on your Adventure Sheet. If you now have three crosses, turn to page 70. As long as you don't yet have three crosses, turn to page 3.

Joe follows them down to the shore on the pretext of collecting driftwood. "Don't go far off," he calls out. "Your aunt says I'm to keep an eye on you."

"What nonsense," says Philip to the others when they are out of Joe's earshot. "He just wants to poke his nose into our business."

Reaching the cave, they wade in through the low dark entrance. Joe watches and then turns around to look for driftwood. He does not think they can get out of the cave without him noticing.

Look at the Adventure Sheet. If there is a tick next to the picture of a key, turn to page 14. If not, turn to page 24.

Dinah takes the tray with her uncle's supper and knocks on the study door. After a long delay, an absent-minded voice grunts, "Enter."

All four walls of the study are covered from floor to ceiling with bookcases and charts. There is only one small gap where the window is. There are more books piled up on the floor, and Dinah has to tread carefully around these looking for a space where she can put down the tray.

Uncle Jocelyn is examining a very old map under a magnifying glass. Dinah looks over his shoulder and says, "That's a map of part of the coast here, isn't it?"

Uncle Jocelyn nodded. "Run along, there's a good girl."

He bends back over his papers, not noticing that Dinah has seen another map showing the Isle of Gloom itself. She pulls it out of the pile of charts and hides it under her jumper. Think how useful it will be! Dinah is certain her uncle won't realize it is missing.

Put a tick next to the picture of a map on the Adventure Sheet. Then turn to page 15.

Jack steers for the gap in the reef. A strong surge of current carries the boat to one side. There is a bump, followed by a dreadful scraping sound along the underside of the hull.

Philip crouches down and inspects the bottom of the boat. "We're lucky. I think we just glanced off a rock."

"It sounded like a close shave, but we're clear of the reef now," says Jack.

Kiki is clutching Jack's shoulder in alarm. "You naughty boy!" she squawks into his ear.

They are safe, but it was still foolhardy to take such a big risk. Put a cross on your Adventure Sheet. If you now have three crosses, turn to page 70. If you still have two or fewer crosses, turn to page 26.

It is not long before they are completely lost in the mines.

"I'm *sure* we came this way," insists Philip, retracing his steps. But he is wrong: there is only a blank wall at the end of the tunnel.

When their candles burn out they are left in total blackness. Lucy-Ann shivers and tries not to let the others know she is crying. Then Dinah thinks she hears voices, somewhere in the distance. They start calling for help, but no one answers.

There is no way to tell how long it is before they hear someone coming. A torchbeam shines out of the dark and a voice calls out: "They're over here!"

With great relief, the children are led to safety by the coastguard. At the top of the shaft they find Bill Smugs waiting for them. He is obviously happy they are all right, but he is also very angry. "I guessed you must have come here," he says. "It's a good thing we found you before you starved. You shouldn't have come, because there was a gang of crooks hiding on this island, and all this fuss has scared them away. We'll never catch them now!"

"Oh dear, Bill," whimpers Lucy-Ann.

Oh dear, indeed! Still, you could try the adventure again and see if you can do any better. First rub out any ticks and crosses on the Adventure Sheet, then turn to page 1.

They come to a dead end and lose valuable time blundering back in the dark to find the side tunnel. Put a cross on your Adventure Sheet. If you now have three crosses, turn immediately to page 70. As long as you don't yet have three crosses, read on.

They see lantern-light from around a bend in the passage and hear a gruff voice saying: "They must've run back up the other way."

They wait silently while listening to footsteps recede down the tunnel. When the coast is clear, Philip leads the way along the side passage and back up the ladder to the surface.

There is no sign of Jack. "He must still be trapped down there," says Dinah. Lucy-Ann cannot help crying; she is worried about her brother.

"We'd better go back to the mainland and get help," decides Philip. Turn to page 18.

Dinah takes the opportunity to ask her uncle if he has any more maps or books relating to the Isle of Gloom.

He sips his cocoa and thinks for a moment. "Not really. There's a book about this house, though. It was used by smugglers hundreds of years ago, and I believe there was a secret tunnel out to the island, right under the sea bed. Smugglers would drop off their contraband on the island, you see, and then bring it ashore secretly, using the tunnel."

Dinah borrows the book and takes it to the sitting room to show the others. Only Bill can read the old script. "It says here that the secret tunnel starts at the bottom of the well!" he says.

"What are we waiting for?" cries Philip, leaping to his feet. "Let's go and rescue Jack!"

"Not so fast," says Bill. "I'm not going down the well in the dead of night. We'll get some sleep first, and take a look at this tunnel first thing tomorrow."

They are all up at the crack of dawn, grabbing a few slices of toast for breakfast before going out to look at the well. Bill spots some rungs leading down the side of the shaft, and starts to climb down. If you think the children should go with him, turn to page 29. If not, turn to page 39.

Before long there is the muffled crump of an explosion, followed by the roar of water pouring into the mines. As water begins to seep under the door and rises up around their ankles, Bill tries to calm them, saying: "The important thing is not to panic."

"But, Bill," wails Dinah, "we're going to drown!"

"No we're not," he tells her. "Look, there'll be a pocket of air under the roof of this room. As long as we can tread water until police divers come to rescue us, we'll be all right."

The water rises steadily. It is horribly cold. Floating up to the ceiling, they all try to use up as little air as possible. The children see that Bill is trying to make the best of the situation, but even he cannot be sure the police will arrive in time.

It is a horrible ordeal, and it seems to go on for hours. They are up to their necks in icy sea water and unable to see a thing. The air seems stifling, and even a deep breath gives very little oxygen. Just as they are on the point of giving up, divers bob up beside them and, holding oxygen masks to their faces, swim with them to safety.

"Well, the crooks got away," says Bill when they are all wrapped in blankets and speeding back home in a motorboat, "but we should be thankful to be alive, at least."

If you want to try the adventure again and see if you can do better, rub out all ticks and crosses on the Adventure Sheet and then turn to page 1.

Jack calls the police, who go out to the island in a motorboat. A few hours later they return with the other children, who are frightened but unhurt.

"We've suspected a gang of crooks was operating in this area for some time," a police officer tells them. "Their hideout was on the island. We've rounded up most of them, but their boss got away. And you'll never guess who the boss was – Joe, your strange handyman!"

That's the end of the adventure. You did quite well in helping to catch the crooks, but you could have done better. If you want to have another go, rub out any ticks and crosses on the Adventure Sheet and turn to page 1.

There are policemen at the top of the shaft. They are holding Joe and his men at gunpoint. Joe glares at Bill and the children. "So you escaped!" he growls. "I can't think how! And tell me, how did the coppers get here in time to catch us?"

Bill laughs. "I called them before setting out for the island, of course."

There are motorboats waiting to take them back to the mainland. Soon everything is explained. Bill is really a Special Branch officer and he has been working undercover in the area for several weeks, trying to catch Joe and his gang of counterfeiters. "Thanks to you, we've got them at last," he says. "You are all heroes."

"Wipe your feet! Where's your handkerchief? Poor old Polly," squawks Kiki.

"Yes, Kiki," says Bill, laughing, "even you!"

THE END

THE ENID BLYTON TRUST
FOR CHILDREN

We hope you have enjoyed the adventures of the children in this book. Please think for a moment about those children who are too ill to do the exciting things you and your friends do.

Help them by sending a donation, large or small, to the ENID BLYTON TRUST FOR CHILDREN. The Trust will use all your gifts to help children who are sick or handicapped and need to be made happy and comfortable.

Please send your postal orders or cheques to:

The Enid Blyton Trust for Children, International House, 1 St Katharine's Way, London E1 9UN

Thank you very much for your help.